Ascens

This is a work of fiction. Similarities to real people, places, or events are entirely coincidental.

ASCENSION

First edition. September 30, 2024.

Copyright © 2024 Edward Heath.

ISBN: 979-8227037749

Written by Edward Heath.

Table of Contents

- Ascension (noun): 1
- Prologue 2
- Chapter 1: After the Storm 4
- Chapter 2: Uneasy Allies 8
- Chapter 3: The Spark of Ascension 14
- Chapter 4: The Return of Malachor 22
- Chapter 5: Shadows Within 26
- Chapter 6: The Price of Power 31
- Chapter 7: The Heart's Sacrifice 33
- Chapter 8: Malachor's Gambit 36
- Chapter 9: The Final Stand 39
- Chapter 10: Aftermath 43
- Epilogue 46

To my family and friends, who have been my guiding light through every shadow. To the readers, who walk this path of light and darkness with me—may you find your own balance in the story's journey. This is for all of you, who believe in the magic within and beyond.

Ascension (noun):

A rare and profound transformation in which a vampire or other supernatural being transcends their original nature, gaining immunity to weaknesses such as sunlight and the need for blood, and becoming a higher, more evolved entity. This process is typically triggered by an act of pure, selfless sacrifice rooted in abiding love or compassion. Ascension grants enhanced physical and spiritual abilities, allowing the being to exist as a bridge between mortal and supernatural realms, while being largely indistinguishable from humans.

Prologue

There were two forces that had always existed, even before the first breath of the universe was drawn: light and shadow. Opposites bound by an ancient balance, they were more than just the difference between day and night. They were woven into the fabric of existence itself, shaping the worlds, the realms, and the beings that inhabited them.

In this universe, the war between light and shadow was not fought with armies on battlefields. It was subtle, quiet, waged in the corners of the mind, in the choices between good and evil, chaos and order. It bled into every corner of creation, threading through mortals and immortals alike, touching everything from the ethereal heights of the celestial planes to the deepest pits of darkness.

For centuries, the balance had held. The forces of light, radiant and pure, held sway over the realms of clarity, hope, and protection. Their influence brought order, but with it, rigidity. The shadows, dark and relentless, thrived in the places beyond the reach of light, fostering chaos, change, and the unknown. In shadow, there was freedom, but also the promise of destruction.

And then there were those who stood at the center of it all—beings who were neither fully one nor the other, but caught between. Mortal and immortal, human and divine, creatures who carried both light and shadow within them, bound by the need to keep the balance. For in this world, power was not inherited but earned through sacrifice, through struggle, through understanding the delicate dance of these forces.

The mortal realm, vast and unaware, rested on the edge of this balance, ignorant of the unseen battles fought around them. Vampires walked the streets, hiding in plain sight, their existence shaped by a dark hunger. Some sought redemption, others power. Celestials, demigods, and beings of old walked among mortals, their divine nature cloaked by the ordinary. Their influence, however, was never far, for they understood that even the smallest shift in the balance could ripple through the realms, tipping the scales dangerously toward destruction.

Yet, the balance was not a static thing. It shifted with each action, each decision made by those who lived within the universe's grasp. There were times when shadow surged, threatening to consume the world in darkness. And times when the light burned too brightly, searing everything in its path.

It was in those moments—when the scales tipped too far in one direction—that chaos would emerge. And with chaos came beings who sought to exploit it, to harness the power of imbalance for their own gain. For those who could control the forces of light and shadow, even for a fleeting moment, could wield unimaginable power.

But with power came consequence. For every rise, there was a fall. For every action, a price to be paid.

The universe, vast and unyielding, continued its silent march forward, watching as the beings within it played their part in the eternal struggle. The balance would always be there—always waiting, always watching, its fragile equilibrium held in the hands of those who understood the truth:

Light cannot exist without shadow, and shadow cannot exist without light. And those who stand between must walk a path few dare to tread, for they carry within them the fate of all worlds.

Chapter 1: After the Storm

Emma stepped closer, her hand finding his, grounding him in the reality of the moment. "What now?"

Kaelith exhaled, a slow, steady breath, his mind finally clear. "Now," he said, his voice filled with certainty, "we move forward."

They stood in silence for a moment, the stillness of the battlefield stretching out before them like a graveyard of decisions made, lives lost, and battles both won and yet to come. The weight of everything Kaelith had done—and everything he was becoming—pressed down on him, heavier than the air around them. Emma's hand, cool and steady, was a reminder of the present, a tether to the world he often felt slipping away from him.

"Forward to what?" Emma's voice was softer now, more a question than a challenge. Her eyes, usually sharp and calculating, softened as they searched his face. She had seen the worst parts of him—the shadow and light battling inside—and still she stayed.

Kaelith's gaze remained fixed on the horizon. "To whatever comes next." His voice was calm, but there was a tremor of uncertainty underneath it. He could no longer pretend to understand the path ahead. The battle had been one thing, but the storm inside him—the constant clash of his angelic and demonic nature—was another. And then there was Malachor, always lurking, waiting for a moment of weakness.

He glanced down at their intertwined hands. Hers so still, so steady. His trembling ever so slightly, though whether from exhaustion or fear, he couldn't be sure.

"You know, you don't have to carry this alone," Emma whispered, her grip tightening just slightly. "We're in this together. I told you that."

Kaelith turned to face her, his expression softening for the briefest of moments. "I know," he said, almost a murmur. His eyes—so often hard and filled with the weight of responsibility—softened as they met hers. "But my burden is not yours to carry. This—" He lifted their joined hands slightly, his voice trailing off as if the words were too heavy to form. "This is something I'm not sure even I can handle."

Emma's brow furrowed. "Don't say that," she replied firmly, her voice cutting through the stillness. "You're stronger than you think. And I'm not going anywhere."

Kaelith gave her a small, strained smile. "That's what I'm afraid of," he admitted. "I don't know what I'll become, Emma. There's something inside me... something dark. And it's growing."

A silence fell between them, thick with unspoken fears. Kaelith turned away, his eyes searching the distant trees, as though the answers to his internal war lay somewhere beyond the shadows. But he knew better. There were no easy answers. Only choices.

"When Malachor comes again," Emma began cautiously, watching him closely, "we'll face him together. Just like before."

He sighed, feeling the exhaustion in his bones. "No, not like before. I'm not the same. I can feel it... shifting. The light and the shadow—they're both getting stronger, and I don't know how long I can keep them in balance." His voice dropped to a near whisper, a hint of fear creeping into the words. "And if I can't—"

"Stop," she interrupted, stepping in front of him, forcing him to look at her. "Stop thinking you're alone in this." Her eyes burned with fierce intensity. "You're not. We'll figure this out together, like we always do."

He let out a shaky breath, rubbing his forehead as though trying to ease the growing tension. "But at what cost, Emma?" His voice cracked with emotion. "What happens when the light consumes me? Or worse, when the shadow does?" He paused, the weight of his fears sinking in. "What happens when I become something you can't stand to look at?"

"I'll still be here," she said simply, her tone unyielding. "No matter what happens. I'm not afraid of you."

Kaelith's gaze dropped to the ground, his expression hardening. "Maybe you should be."

A gust of wind swept across the clearing, rustling the leaves in the nearby trees, carrying with it the cold sting of what was to come. Kaelith shivered, though it wasn't the wind that chilled him. It was the creeping realization that the fight inside him—between light and shadow—was far from over.

Emma took a deep breath, her eyes scanning the horizon before returning to Kaelith. "We can't keep standing here waiting for something to happen. If we're moving forward, we need a plan."

Kaelith nodded, though his mind still felt clouded. "Malachor won't stay hidden forever. He's waiting, watching. He'll come for us when we're weakest."

"Then we'll make sure we're not," Emma replied, her voice steady. "But you need rest. We both do. You're not thinking clearly, and if we go looking for a fight like this..." She trailed off, shaking her head. "It'll kill us both."

Kaelith didn't argue. He was too tired to. The exhaustion went beyond the physical—it was in his soul. A deep, aching weariness from trying to hold together two opposing forces within him. He squeezed Emma's hand again, grateful for her presence, even if he didn't believe her words entirely.

"We'll rest," he agreed softly. "But not for long."

Emma nodded, pulling him gently toward the shelter of the nearby trees. "I'll stand watch tonight. You need to sleep."

Kaelith looked at her, the shadows under his eyes darkening as he fought back against the weight of everything that had happened. "You should rest too, Emma. You've done more than enough."

She gave him a faint smile, though it didn't quite reach her eyes. "You forget," she said, voice light, though her expression was far from it, "I'm a vampire. I don't need sleep the way you do."

Kaelith allowed himself a small, weary chuckle at that. "Right. Of course." But as they moved under the trees, he couldn't shake the nagging thought that rest would do little to ease the storm that was still raging inside him.

As the night fell and the darkness closed in around them, Kaelith settled onto the ground, his head resting against the base of a tree. The wind howled in the distance, a reminder of the battles yet to come, but for the moment, there was only the sound of Emma's soft breathing and the quiet rustle of leaves.

Sleep tugged at the edges of his consciousness, but his mind was still spinning, unable to fully relax. He thought of Malachor, lurking in the shadows, biding his time. And he thought of Emma, her unwavering presence, always there to pull him back from the brink.

But as his eyes began to close, another thought crept in. A darker thought.

What if, next time, he didn't come back?

Chapter 2: Uneasy Allies

Morning was creeping over the horizon, its pale light slowly casting long shadows through the trees. Emma felt the tension in her body rise with each passing moment. She had only a short window before the sunlight became lethal, and they were still exposed out in the open.

"We have to move," she whispered urgently, shaking Kaelith awake from his restless sleep.

Kaelith stirred, blinking as the morning light began to filter through the leaves. "What's wrong?"

Emma glanced at the brightening sky, her voice tight with urgency. "Sunlight. It'll kill me if we don't get to cover."

Kaelith nodded, shaking off the sleep and pushing himself to his feet. He could feel Emma's anxiety through the tension in her voice, and though his body was still weary from their last battle, he forced himself to move. "Where can we go?"

"I've got a small apartment near my parents' loft. We can get there before the sun breaks fully."

The two of them hurried through the thinning forest, their footsteps quiet but quick. The unspoken tension between them weighed heavily in the silence, made even more tangible by the circumstances they found themselves in. Kaelith's thoughts were a jumble—his power, still untamed, felt like a coiled force inside him, and it was getting harder to control. The balance between light and shadow had become more delicate, more fragile with each fight, each moment of stress.

But Emma—she was different. Her struggle was clear to him now: she was **hungry**. The gnawing need for blood was growing stronger in her, and while she remained composed, Kaelith could sense the mounting pressure.

They made it to Emma's apartment just as the sun broke fully over the horizon. The windows were shielded with heavy drapes, protecting her from the light that now streamed across the city. Inside, the atmosphere was calm but laden with unspoken fears.

Emma let out a small sigh of relief, sinking into the chair near the door. "Barely made it," she muttered, her eyes closing briefly as she tried to shake off the tension.

Kaelith stayed standing, his eyes scanning the room absently as if searching for something, though he knew not what. His mind was too preoccupied with the **sense of unease** that had settled over him since their last confrontation with Malachor. The silence between them was no longer comfortable; it was heavy with unspoken truths, fears, and uncertainties that neither of them had yet voiced.

"You can rest," Emma said softly, noticing the exhaustion in his posture. "We're safe for now."

Kaelith nodded but didn't move. He was still grappling with the same question that had haunted him since the battle: *What was happening to him?* The **powers within him**—the light, the shadow—were becoming more unpredictable, harder to control, and more draining with every use. He wasn't sure how much longer he could keep balancing them, or if he even wanted to.

"It's not just Malachor, is it?" Emma's voice broke through his thoughts, bringing him back to the present.

Kaelith turned to her, meeting her gaze. "No, it's not." His voice was low, almost a whisper. He walked over to the window, glancing outside as if he could see beyond the buildings, beyond the horizon, to the danger that lurked there. "It's me. I'm changing, Emma. And I don't know what I'm becoming."

Emma stood and approached him cautiously. "You're still you, Kaelith," she said firmly. "Whatever's happening, whatever you're feeling—it doesn't change that."

He shook his head, his hands clenching into fists at his sides. "You don't understand," he muttered, his voice thick with frustration. "Every time I use my powers, it drains me. I'm... losing control."

Her hand touched his arm, pulling him back from the edge of his thoughts. "Then we'll figure it out. Together." She sounded so certain, so steady, and he almost believed her. But deep down, he knew the truth—there was something inside him that couldn't be figured out. Not like this.

"What happens when I can't hold it back anymore?" he asked, his voice strained. "What happens when the shadow takes over?"

"You won't let that happen," Emma replied softly, though her expression was tense. "I won't let that happen."

Kaelith sighed, rubbing his temples as if trying to soothe the storm inside his mind. "It's getting harder," he admitted. "And Malachor... I can feel him out there. He's waiting for me to break."

Emma's eyes darkened at the mention of Malachor. "The council's been on high alert ever since the rumors started," she said. "They've been tracking every lead, but they're terrified. They know Malachor won't stop until he gets what he wants."

Kaelith turned to face her fully, his expression hardening. "Then we have to stop him before that happens. We can't keep waiting for him to make the first move."

Emma frowned, glancing away as if weighing her next words carefully. "The council is working on it. But right now, we need to be smart. And you..." She trailed off, her gaze flicking toward him briefly before returning to the floor. "You need rest. You're no good to anyone if you keep pushing yourself like this."

He opened his mouth to protest, but she cut him off, her tone firm. "You're not invincible, Kaelith. You can't fight Malachor if you're running on empty."

Kaelith stared at her, his jaw tight, but he knew she was right. The truth was, he had been running on fumes ever since their last battle, and the strain was starting to show. But it wasn't just physical exhaustion—it was the weight of the unknown. The uncertainty about what was happening to him, what he was becoming.

He exhaled slowly, nodding. "You're right," he said, his voice low. "But we can't stay hidden forever."

"We won't," Emma assured him, her gaze softening slightly. "But we need time. Time to figure out what's happening to you. And time for me to..." She hesitated, her eyes flickering with something he couldn't quite place.

Kaelith raised an eyebrow, sensing her hesitation. "To what?"

Emma sighed, crossing her arms tightly over her chest. "I need to feed, Kaelith. Soon. If I don't..."

Her voice trailed off, but she didn't need to finish the sentence. He knew what would happen if she went too long without feeding. The hunger would consume her, and she would lose control.

Kaelith's expression softened as he stepped closer. "How long has it been?"

"Too long," she admitted, her voice barely a whisper. "But I can't think about that right now. We have bigger problems."

"No, Emma," he said firmly, his eyes narrowing with concern. "This is important. You can't keep ignoring it."

She flinched at the truth in his words, her body tightening. "I know." She hesitated, frustration lacing her tone. "But what am I supposed to do? Go find some stranger or criminal? Become just another vampire feeding in the dark?"

Kaelith frowned, understanding her reluctance. The thought of Emma being reduced to that, of having to take life or degrade herself for survival, pained him. After a moment, a thought crossed his mind. He hesitated briefly, then rolled up his sleeve and extended his wrist to her. "Take mine."

Emma's eyes widened in shock. She stared at his offered wrist, her breath catching in her throat. The pulse beneath his skin thrummed with life, and her hunger roared to life at the sight of it. She could almost feel the warmth of his blood before even touching him, the need surging in her veins.

But she didn't move.

"Emma, you need to feed," Kaelith urged softly. "And I'm offering. It's fine. I trust you."

She took a step back, shaking her head. "No," she said, her voice trembling. "Not from you."

Kaelith's brow furrowed in confusion. "Why not? You need blood, and I'm—"

"It's different," she interrupted, her voice sharp, though not from anger. Her hands clenched at her sides as she struggled to find the words. "Strangers, criminals, blood dolls—that's one thing. But this—" She looked at him, her eyes softening as they met his. "This is you, Kaelith. It's too personal. Too... intimate."

Kaelith blinked, surprised. "Intimate? Emma, I'm offering this because I want to help you. There's nothing... romantic about it."

She looked away, unable to meet his gaze. "Maybe not for you," she whispered. "But for me... it's different. Taking your blood... it's not just survival. It's too close. I—" She hesitated, her voice faltering. "I don't deserve that."

Kaelith took a step forward, his voice gentle. "You don't deserve it? Emma, you're not a monster. You're not unworthy of anything."

Her eyes met his again, filled with a sadness he hadn't seen before. "You don't understand. You're... you're different. You're divine. I can't taint that."

Kaelith lowered his arm, his heart heavy as he realized how deep her fear ran. Slowly, he stepped closer, his hand resting lightly on her shoulder. "You won't taint anything, Emma," he said softly. "But if you don't want this... I won't force it. Just know that you're not unworthy. Not to me."

She nodded, her body trembling slightly as she held back the hunger. "Thank you," she whispered, turning away to hide the emotions that had welled up inside her. "But I can't. Not now. I'll... I'll figure something else out."

Kaelith watched her for a long moment, the tension between them hanging in the air. He wanted to push, to insist that she didn't have to hide her needs from him, but he knew when to pull back. For now, he would respect her decision, even if it hurt him to see her suffer.

"I'll help you any way I can, Emma," he said quietly, stepping back to give her space. "Whenever you're ready."

She nodded, still facing away from him, her voice barely a whisper. "I know."

The air between them was thick with unspoken emotions—Kaelith's willingness to sacrifice anything for her and Emma's refusal to accept it. The tension was palpable, yet beneath it lay an undeniable connection that neither of them were ready to confront just yet.

Over the next few days, they prepared to visit the vampire council. Kaelith felt his strength slipping with each passing hour, and Emma's hunger gnawed at her constantly. Tensions rose, and though they were united in their purpose, the complications of their natures threatened to drive a wedge between them.

The vampire council was on high alert. Malachor's crimes—unforgivable and growing in legend—cast a long shadow over every meeting and decision. Emma, still hiding her growing hunger, knew that if they didn't act soon, they might not get another chance. And if Malachor struck while Kaelith was weak... it could be the end for both of them.

Chapter 3: The Spark of Ascension

Evening fell again, blanketing the city in shadow. Emma had returned from feeding, her hunger satiated for the time being, but Kaelith's restlessness had only grown. His powers were slipping further from his grasp, and no amount of reflection or meditation could seem to fix it.

"You need help," Emma had said, more firm than usual.

And now they were standing before the sanctuary of William Priest, an ancient being rumored to be as old as the druids. Emma knocked on the door of the unassuming building. Moments later, the door creaked open, revealing a dimly lit space filled with the scent of herbs, parchment, and wood smoke.

A man stood in the doorway—tall, lean, with an ageless quality to his face, eyes sharp and wise beyond anything Kaelith had ever encountered. William Priest.

"Emma," William greeted, his voice like gravel over stone. He glanced at Kaelith. "And who do we have here?"

"This is Kaelith," Emma said, her tone more respectful than usual. "He's... in need of your help."

William's gaze lingered on Kaelith, piercing. He didn't speak for a long moment, and Kaelith felt as though William was looking straight through him, unraveling his secrets.

"And why would you need my help, Kaelith?" William finally asked, his voice neutral but inquisitive.

Kaelith felt the weight of William's stare but met his eyes. "I'm... losing control," he said slowly, struggling to find the right words. "I'm not sure what's happening, but my powers are... changing. The balance between light and shadow is slipping."

William's eyebrows rose slightly. "Light and shadow?" he repeated, stepping aside and motioning them in. "Interesting."

They entered the sanctuary, the warmth of the room a sharp contrast to the cold outside. Books and ancient relics filled the space, and the walls were lined with symbols Kaelith didn't recognize. William gestured for them to sit, but Kaelith remained standing, his discomfort palpable.

William didn't press him. Instead, he crossed the room and took a seat in an old wooden chair. "Tell me more," he said. "When did this imbalance begin?"

Kaelith frowned, thinking back. "After the battle with Malachor. It started small—like I couldn't quite keep the light and shadow separate anymore. But lately, it's been getting worse. When I use one, the other pushes back harder."

William nodded, listening carefully. "That's to be expected," he murmured. "The more you rely on one side, the more the other will resist. They are two forces within you, both demanding to be heard."

Kaelith crossed his arms, frustration creeping into his voice. "But I've been balancing them my whole life. Why is it falling apart now?"

William's eyes narrowed slightly, considering. "Because you're not the same man you were before, Kaelith. Something has changed in you. Something deeper than just the fight with Malachor."

"What are you suggesting?" Kaelith asked, though he had a sinking feeling that he already knew.

"You're becoming more than what you were," William said simply. "The power inside you is growing. Evolving. And with that evolution comes instability. You're holding onto what you were, rather than embracing what you are now."

Kaelith clenched his fists at his sides. "What am I supposed to be, then? I'm not... I don't want to become something I can't control."

William leaned forward, resting his elbows on his knees. "Tell me, Kaelith—how often do you use your powers? Not just in battle, but in the quiet moments. Do you push them away? Do you let yourself truly feel what you are?"

Kaelith hesitated. "I... I try to control it. To keep it balanced."

"Control is one thing," William said, his voice firm. "But suppression is another. You cannot suppress one side of yourself without weakening the other. You need to let both sides breathe, to coexist without fear."

Kaelith's jaw tightened. "That's easier said than done."

William smiled faintly. "It always is."

The days bled into nights, and the nights were filled with training. Weeks passed as Kaelith worked with William, trying to understand the balance between his light and shadow. Emma stayed nearby, watching the transformation slowly take shape. The process was grueling—mentally, emotionally, and physically.

William was patient but persistent. "You're still holding back," he would say during their sessions. "You fear the shadow. But it is as much a part of you as the light. You need to stop thinking of them as enemies."

"I'm not holding back," Kaelith had argued more than once. "I'm trying to keep control."

"And there's your problem," William would reply. "It's not about control. It's about acceptance."

Kaelith's frustration grew, but so did his awareness of the forces inside him. He could feel the light within him burning brighter than before, but with each flare of light, the shadow seemed to grow darker, more pronounced. The two sides fought for dominance, and it was only through William's guidance that Kaelith was beginning to understand how to stop that constant tug-of-war.

One evening, after a particularly intense training session, Kaelith stood by the window, looking out into the dark. Emma approached him, her presence steady.

"You're getting better," she said softly. "I can see it."

Kaelith shook his head. "I'm not sure. It feels like I'm walking on a knife's edge. One wrong move, and it all falls apart."

Emma rested a hand on his shoulder. "You won't let that happen."

Kaelith's gaze remained on the distant city. "I hope you're right."

As they walked through a dimly lit alleyway, Emma's senses tingled with the awareness that something was wrong. She instinctively stepped closer to Kaelith, her sharp eyes scanning the darkness ahead.

"Something's here," she whispered, her tone tense.

Before either of them could react, a blur of movement shot out from the shadows—a vampire, wild-eyed and desperate with hunger. He lunged directly at Kaelith, mistaking him for a mortal, unaware of his true nature or Emma's presence.

Emma moved, but the vampire was too fast. His fangs sank into Kaelith's neck before she could intervene.

Kaelith gasped, his body going rigid from the sudden shock of the bite. He could feel the vampire drawing deeply on his blood, but something inside him stirred. His divine essence, raw and powerful, reacted violently to the assault. The air around them seemed to hum with energy, and the vampire, still feeding, froze as the divine blood coursed through his veins.

The vampire's eyes widened in shock. His body began to glow faintly, a soft radiance pulsing under his skin. The hunger that had driven him moments before faded entirely, replaced by a sudden rush of strength. He staggered back from Kaelith, ripping his fangs free, and stumbled, staring at his hands as if they belonged to someone else.

Kaelith collapsed to his knees, clutching his neck as the wound quickly sealed itself, his divine blood working its way through his body. He felt drained, his energy sapped, but he managed to look up, disoriented.

The vampire, still glowing faintly, stood there, wide-eyed. His movements were sharper, more controlled, and as the faint light washed over him, he didn't recoil in pain—it seemed to invigorate him instead.

Emma rushed to Kaelith's side, her eyes flicking between him and the transformed vampire. "Kaelith... what just happened?"

Kaelith tried to speak, but his voice was weak, barely above a whisper. "I... I don't know."

The vampire, still staring in disbelief at his own body, looked toward them. "The hunger... it's gone," he muttered, almost in awe. "The light... it doesn't hurt."

Emma's expression darkened with understanding. "Kaelith... your blood. It triggered something in him. You've... sparked an ascension."

Kaelith's heart pounded in his chest as Emma's words sunk in. The realization hit him like a blow. His divine blood had transformed the vampire, albeit temporarily, granting him immunity to both hunger and light. He hadn't meant for this to happen—it had been an accident, a reaction he didn't even know was possible.

"We need to leave," Emma urged, grabbing Kaelith's arm. "Now."

She helped him to his feet, her gaze wary of the vampire, who still stood motionless, processing the change. His skin no longer glowed, the brief ascension already fading, but the effects lingered.

"Go," the vampire said quietly, his voice filled with a strange reverence. "I won't stop you."

Emma didn't need any further encouragement. She pulled Kaelith along, the weight of the situation hanging heavily between them. They hurried through the alley, putting distance between themselves and the vampire, unsure of what had just been set in motion.

The sanctuary was quiet when they arrived, the door creaking open as William stepped out to greet them. His eyes immediately narrowed as he saw Kaelith's weakened state and the troubled look on Emma's face.

"What happened?" William asked, his voice calm but probing.

Kaelith, still unsteady, leaned against Emma, his breath labored. "A vampire... attacked me."

William's expression darkened. "And?"

Kaelith winced, still reeling from the experience. "He fed on me. And when he did, something changed. He didn't burn in the light, and his hunger... it vanished."

William's gaze sharpened as he glanced between Kaelith and Emma. "Your blood. Your divine nature."

Emma nodded, her voice filled with urgency. "He didn't realize what Kaelith was. He fed, and it sparked something in him. An ascension."

William crossed the room, his face grim. "That's dangerous. Very dangerous." He turned to Kaelith. "Your blood carries the essence of divinity. Vampires, feeding off it... they could be changed—ascended, like this one. If others find out about this..."

Kaelith's stomach churned. He hadn't known that his blood could have such an effect, but now it was clear. The implications were terrifying.

Emma looked at William, her voice steady but tense. "It's not just that vampire. I... I felt something too. Being near Kaelith... the hunger, it fades. I don't know why, but it does."

William's expression grew more serious. "It's the divine energy within him. It affects vampires, perhaps not as strongly as direct feeding, but it's still a force. Kaelith, you are more dangerous than you realize. And if this gets out..."

Kaelith, still weak, stared at the floor, his mind racing with the consequences of what had just occurred. This wasn't just about learning to control his powers anymore. There was something far greater at stake now—something he wasn't sure he could handle.

News of Kaelith's unintentional spark spread through the vampire community like wildfire. Rumors circulated that he held the power to grant ascension—an ability most vampires could only dream of. Whispers of the miracle spread through every dark corner of the city, and soon, it wasn't just talk. Vampires began showing up at William's sanctuary, their desperation palpable.

Some came pleading, eyes wide with hope, begging for Kaelith's blood to free them from their hunger. Others came with darker intentions—threats laced in their words, warning him of the consequences if he didn't share his gift.

Kaelith, still reeling from the strain of his powers, found himself trapped in a storm he hadn't anticipated. His every action was scrutinized, his sanctuary invaded by the endless requests for ascension. Each time he refused, the weight grew heavier. His energy drained with every encounter, his connection to the divine and shadow wavering under the pressure.

But not all vampires sought to use him. The Vampire Council, the ruling body that governed their kind, took notice of the rumors. Unlike the others, the Council understood the magnitude of what was happening. While many vampires—council members included—longed to be free of the eternal hunger and the curse of the light, they knew the cost of demanding such a gift from Kaelith was far too high.

In a rare meeting, Kaelith stood before the Council. The most powerful vampires in the city regarded him with both reverence and wariness, recognizing the delicate balance his presence created.

"This gift you possess," one of the council members spoke, his voice measured and firm, "it is a power that many in our community would kill for. But we recognize the toll it takes on you."

Another council member, an older vampire with deep-set eyes, nodded. "We do not wish to see you used, Kaelith. You are an ally to our kind, not a tool to be exploited for personal gain."

The tension in the room was thick as Kaelith, exhausted from the constant demands and the heavy weight of his abilities, spoke. "I never wanted this," he admitted quietly. "I don't even fully understand what I've done or how to stop it."

The head of the Council, a tall, commanding figure, stepped forward. "We will ensure that your privacy is respected," he said firmly. "This power is too dangerous for any one being to wield freely. Those who come seeking ascension will be turned away, and those who defy this command will face the consequences."

Despite their assurances, Kaelith couldn't shake the growing sense of dread. Even with the Council's protection, the knowledge of what his blood could do had already spread too far. There would always be those who sought him, willing to stop at nothing to claim his power for themselves.

And through it all, the threat of Malachor loomed larger than ever.

The darkness surrounding Malachor had grown in the background, waiting patiently, feeding off the chaos that had been created. Kaelith could feel it—like a shadow creeping closer with each passing day. The whispers of vampires seeking ascension were not the only rumors that circulated. Word of Kaelith's divine power had reached Malachor, and now the ancient enemy was preparing to make his move.

Malachor knew that Kaelith was weakened, and the storm that had been brewing in the distance was finally about to crash over them all.

As Kaelith left the council chambers, Emma walked beside him, her expression tight with concern. "The Council's on your side," she said softly. "That's something."

Kaelith nodded, though his mind was far from at ease. "It won't be enough. Not with Malachor out there."

Emma glanced at him, her voice dropping to a whisper. "Do you think he knows?"

Kaelith's eyes darkened as he looked out into the night. "He does now."

The storm had finally arrived, and this time, Kaelith wasn't sure if he could weather it.

Chapter 4: The Return of Malachor

Malachor, sensing Kaelith's weakened state after triggering the ascension, begins to resurface. He manipulates those around Kaelith, preying on their desires and fears, using Kaelith's diminished power to create chaos. Malachor's influence spreads quietly at first, whispers in the night, but soon it becomes clear that he is making his move. His reach extends to both Kaelith and Emma, and the attacks begin.

One evening, while Kaelith and Emma return from training with William, a group of vampires strikes. Their eyes burn with the corruption of Malachor's influence. Emma fights them off, but Kaelith struggles. Every time he uses his abilities, it drains him more and more. The divine power inside him no longer flows as smoothly as it once did, and the balance between his light and shadow continues to shift, pulling him in different directions. The attacks grow more frequent, and Emma can see how much it is wearing on him.

Despite the danger, Emma remains by his side, unwilling to let him face it alone. Her bond with Kaelith strengthens, though neither of them speak openly about their feelings. They share quiet moments during the aftermath of the battles, but those moments are fleeting, overshadowed by the threat that Malachor poses. Emma's parents, Alex and Aurelia, watch their daughter closely. Aurelia, in particular, teases Emma about the way she looks at Kaelith.

"You've got that look in your eyes, the one I had when I first met Alex," Aurelia says with a knowing smile. "You're not as subtle as you think."

Emma brushes it off, but her mother's words stay with her. Aurelia's teasing is light-hearted, but beneath it, there is truth. Emma feels herself being pulled closer to Kaelith, even as the danger around them grows.

Meanwhile, the Vampire Council becomes increasingly involved. They summon Kaelith to discuss the growing unrest in the vampire community. The council members understand the appeal of what Kaelith represents: a chance to escape the curse of hunger and walk in the daylight. But they also see the cost it takes on him, and they know that such power comes with great danger. In the meeting, the Council reminds the vampires of the first Vampire War, a conflict that nearly destroyed both their world and the mortal realm.

The war began when vampires sought powers beyond their nature, leading to a violent struggle for control. Mortals became aware of the immortal world, and chaos followed. It took centuries for the balance to be restored, but not before countless lives were lost on both sides. The Council warns that if vampires continue to seek ascension from Kaelith, they risk reigniting a similar conflict. They issue a decree, urging all vampires to respect Kaelith's privacy and treat him as an ally, not a tool to be exploited for their own gain.

Even with the Council's protection, Kaelith knows the situation is spiraling out of control. Vampires still follow him at a distance, some acting as bodyguards on behalf of the Council, others watching him for different reasons. The strain of constantly being pursued takes its toll, and the more he uses his powers, the more vulnerable he becomes.

His training with William continues, but the lessons are becoming harder to absorb. Kaelith feels as though he is caught in a storm, with no way to control the forces inside him. William, though patient, sees the toll it is taking. He urges Kaelith to find balance, but Kaelith is unsure if balance is even possible anymore.

The attacks escalate. Malachor's influence spreads like a disease, and more vampires begin to show up, driven by the dark promises Malachor offers them. Emma does her best to keep Kaelith grounded, but even she can see that he is slipping. The bond between them grows stronger, though neither speaks of it. It is an unspoken connection, a trust that is built in the midst of battle. But it is also fragile, and Emma worries that it may not be enough to save them.

In a rare moment of respite, as Emma and Kaelith sit in the sanctuary after another brutal skirmish, Aurelia visits. She watches her daughter and Kaelith closely, the hint of a smile on her lips.

"You know, Emma, your father and I can see it," Aurelia says, her tone playful but filled with affection. "You and Kaelith are getting close."

Emma rolls her eyes, trying to dismiss her mother's teasing, but Aurelia continues. "It's not a bad thing, you know. The two of you make a good team. Maybe more."

Emma doesn't respond, but the conversation lingers in her mind. Aurelia's teasing might have been light, but Emma can't shake the feelings growing inside her.

As the tension mounts, Kaelith realizes that Malachor is not just toying with him—he is preparing for something larger. The attacks are not random. They are targeted, designed to weaken Kaelith further, to break him before the final confrontation. Emma notices the pattern too, and her worry deepens. She knows Malachor well enough to understand that this is only the beginning.

The final blow comes when Malachor, in the form of a shadowy figure, reveals himself from a distance during one of the ambushes. His presence is a dark reminder of what is coming. Malachor doesn't need to fight Kaelith directly yet. He only needs to wait for the right moment, when Kaelith's strength is all but gone.

Malachor's appearance sends ripples of fear through the vampires. Even those loyal to the Council can feel the weight of his power, and they know what it means. Malachor is back, and his plans are already in motion.

Kaelith, his body and mind exhausted from the constant strain, knows the inevitable is approaching. He can feel the storm gathering, and this time, he may not be ready for what's coming.

Chapter 5: Shadows Within

Kaelith's sleep had become a battleground, one he couldn't escape. Each night, the visions of Damu grew stronger. In these dreams, Damu stood at the heart of a storm, commanding terrifying power—a demigod, whose divine blood was the source of vampirism. The line between Damu and Kaelith blurred, and each time Kaelith woke, it was with the unsettling feeling that he was no longer just himself—he was something more, something ancient.

The visions came without mercy. They reflected the warnings William had been giving him all along: in order to survive and control his powers, Kaelith had to stop denying the truth of his duality. He had to embrace his divine blood and the darkness within him. But doing so felt like surrendering to chaos, and every time Kaelith woke, his heart pounded with fear—fear of what would happen if he fully embraced the force inside him. Fear of becoming Damu.

The weight of these dreams bled into Kaelith's days. His training with William grew more intense, but so did his frustration. Every lesson left him more exhausted than the last. William pushed him hard, urging him to stop resisting.

"You're fighting against yourself, Kaelith," William said one evening after a grueling session. "The divine blood in you and your shadow are not enemies. If you continue treating them that way, they will tear you apart."

Kaelith's jaw clenched. "You're asking me to embrace something I don't fully understand. What if I can't control it?"

"You won't control it by fear," William said calmly, stepping closer. "You need to let go of this idea that you can suppress one side and favor the other. You must embrace both, or neither will serve you."

Kaelith lowered his gaze, uncertain. The visions of Damu had only made things more confusing. He wanted to argue with William, but he couldn't. The visions were proving William's point—Damu's power had come from fully embracing his divine blood and the darkness it brought with it. But that kind of power frightened Kaelith more than he wanted to admit.

William's voice softened. "There's something else I need to tell you, something you might not know yet." Kaelith looked up, waiting. "Those who are divinely touched, like you, or even celestials and demigods... they can never truly die. When their bodies perish, their spirits go to limbo for a time. And then, they're reborn."

Kaelith stared at him, the words heavy in the air. "Reborn?"

"Yes," William said. "It's possible Damu's spirit has been reborn into you. That's why these visions haunt you. You are connected, whether you like it or not."

The revelation hit Kaelith hard. The idea that Damu's spirit had somehow merged with his own was overwhelming. Was he just a vessel for Damu's rebirth? Or was this power his to claim in his own right?

"That's what these visions are," William continued. "They're not just dreams. They're fragments of a past life, urging you to embrace the power you're capable of."

Kaelith's head spun. "And if I don't?"

"You'll never control it," William said bluntly. "And you'll never understand who or what you truly are."

Meanwhile, Emma had noticed the change in Kaelith. His demeanor had grown more distant, more withdrawn, even though they continued to fight side by side during the increasing vampire incursions. The attacks had grown more frequent, and Malachor's influence more apparent with each passing night. Emma, ever the warrior, fought fiercely, but she could see that Kaelith was struggling—both physically and emotionally.

One night, after a brutal ambush, Kaelith and Emma returned to the sanctuary, both covered in cuts and bruises. Emma had dispatched the attackers swiftly, but Kaelith had hesitated. His powers, normally sharp and controlled, had flared unpredictably during the fight. The light he conjured seared the vampires, but the shadow that followed nearly consumed them both.

"Talk to me," Emma said, her voice breaking the silence as they sat near the fire, nursing their wounds. "You've been distant. You're keeping something from me."

Kaelith stared into the flames, the orange light flickering across his face. "It's nothing."

"It's not nothing," Emma insisted, her hand resting on his. "You can't shut me out like this, not now. You're trying to carry too much alone."

Kaelith exhaled, his breath shaky. "If I embrace what's inside me, I don't know if I'll survive it. I don't know if I'll be me anymore."

Emma's brow furrowed. "You think I don't understand that fear? Every day, I live with the possibility that the hunger could overwhelm me, that I'll lose control and become a monster. But I don't let it define me. You're stronger than you think."

He looked at her, a flicker of gratitude in his eyes, but the fear still lingered. "If I lose control, people will die. You could die."

"I trust you," Emma said, her voice firm. "And I need you to trust yourself."

As the days passed, Aurelia and Alex continued to watch their daughter's growing attachment to Kaelith. They, too, had noticed the change in him, the way the weight of his powers was pushing him to the brink. One afternoon, as Emma and Kaelith returned to the sanctuary, Aurelia couldn't help but tease her daughter.

"You're always with him these days," Aurelia remarked with a playful smile. "It's almost like you're his personal bodyguard."

Emma rolled her eyes, but Aurelia pressed on. "You can pretend all you want, but Alex and I see what's going on between you two."

"Nothing's going on, Mother," Emma said, brushing off the comment.

Aurelia raised an eyebrow, her smile deepening. "Sure, sure. Keep telling yourself that."

Despite her teasing, Aurelia understood the bond between Emma and Kaelith, and the deeper concern that lay behind her playful remarks. Kaelith wasn't just fighting against Malachor's forces—he was fighting against himself. And she knew that if he didn't find balance soon, the consequences could be dire.

The Council had been aware of Kaelith's escalating struggle, but their attention was now turning to a greater issue—the direct attacks from Malachor's forces. They summoned Kaelith and Emma to the chamber, hoping to address both the safety of the city and Kaelith's role within it. The Council members, ancient and powerful, watched him closely as he approached, their faces grim.

"You've become a focal point of our world," one of the elders said. "Many seek you out for the power you carry, but they do not understand the cost it takes on you."

Kaelith nodded, the weight of their gaze heavy. "I never wanted this power. I don't even fully understand it."

Another council member, an older vampire with deep-set eyes, spoke up. "That power, if misused, could destroy everything."

The room grew quiet, the elder's words hanging in the air. Malachor's presence was growing, and it was clear that a confrontation was inevitable. But Kaelith wasn't ready, and the Council knew it.

"We will protect you from those who seek to exploit you," the elder said, his voice grave. "But you must find a way to control the forces within you before they consume you."

Kaelith nodded again, but inside, he felt the growing weight of his responsibility. Malachor's attacks were becoming more frequent, and the time for a final confrontation was approaching. He could feel it. The visions of Damu had shown him what he could become, but the cost of that power haunted him.

The attacks continued. Malachor's allies grew bolder, striking at Kaelith and Emma with greater frequency. Each battle left Kaelith more drained, more uncertain. Even William noticed the toll it was taking. During one particularly brutal ambush, Kaelith unleashed a torrent of both light and shadow, the forces ripping through the vampires like a storm. But as the dust settled, Kaelith collapsed, barely conscious, his body trembling from the strain.

Emma knelt beside him, her eyes filled with concern. "You can't keep doing this."

Kaelith struggled to breathe, his voice barely a whisper. "I don't have a choice."

"You do," she said, her grip on his hand tightening. "But you're running out of time to make it."

Chapter 6: The Price of Power

Tensions in the vampire world were at a breaking point. Whispers of rebellion and betrayal echoed through the streets, pointing to a third vampire war that threatened to spill out into the Mortal Realm once again. The memories of past conflicts lingered in every dark corner; no one knew how the mortals would react this time to a second incursion fueled by greed and misunderstandings.

In the midst of this brewing storm, Malachor made a bold move. He kidnapped Emma, holding her hostage to lure Kaelith into a trap. The air was thick with tension, and Kaelith felt something was off but hadn't anticipated this desperate act. Now, Emma was in Malachor's clutches, and Kaclith was faced with a heart-wrenching dilemma.

Kaelith, now deeply conflicted, understood the gravity of his decision. He could use his powers to spark ascension in Emma, potentially giving her protection from his celestial light, or he could keep her safe by maintaining his distance. Malachor, ever cunning, planned to exploit this choice, manipulating their emotions and pushing Kaelith towards a precipice of dangerous decisions.

The night Kaelith decided to confront Malachor, he embraced his full celestial nature for the first time in his life. As he transformed, his form became a perfect embodiment of both light and shadow. Wings of both light and darkness unfurled from his back, his body glowing with an ethereal presence. His eyes emanated pure light, embodying the duality of a demon and an angel fused into one. This was the true form of a celestial being—majestic and terrifying.

As Kaelith entered Malachor's lair, the intense light that radiated from him affected every vampire in the vicinity. The brightness was not merely a visual spectacle; it burned, searing any vampire flesh it touched, including Malachor's. The vampires hissed and recoiled, their skins smoking under the celestial light. Malachor, caught by surprise by the intensity of Kaelith's power, struggled to maintain his composure.

In the chaos, Kaelith reached Emma. She was bound, her body weakened from captivity, her spirit flickering like a flame in the wind. As Kaelith unleashed his power to subdue Malachor and his minions, the uncontrolled light surged brighter than he intended. It enveloped Emma, the unintended casualty of his celestial wrath. The light, pure and overwhelming, was too much for her. Emma's skin blistered and burned as if caught in the sun's unforgiving rays.

With Malachor momentarily subdued, Kaelith scooped Emma into his arms, her body limp and painfully scorched by his light. The battle had taken a dire turn, and now he had to save her life. He fled from the lair, the sounds of chaos fading behind him as he carried Emma to the only safe haven he knew—Alex and Aurelia's loft.

As he ran, Kaelith's mind raced with fear and regret. His first true unleashing of his celestial power had nearly destroyed the one person he had sworn to protect. He burst into the loft, the desperation clear on his face as Alex and Aurelia rushed to aid their daughter.

"She's been hurt by the light," Kaelith gasped out, his voice choked with guilt. "I didn't... I couldn't control it."

Alex and Aurelia sprang into action, their years of dealing with supernatural injuries guiding their hands as they tended to Emma. The severity of her burns was daunting, and the room filled with a tense silence, broken only by the soft murmurs of her pain.

Kaelith stood back, watching helplessly as they worked to stabilize her. The reality of his power and its consequences had never been clearer. As he watched Emma fighting for her life, the weight of his celestial legacy bore down on him. He had become a being of immense power, but at what cost?

Chapter 7: The Heart's Sacrifice

As Kaelith grappled with the aftermath of his unleashed powers, the loft was a flurry of urgent activity. Aurelia and Alex, with decades of experience in handling supernatural crises, administered their aid to Emma with precise and swift movements. The gravity of her condition was reflected in their focused expressions, each motion measured to stabilize her severe injuries.

Kaelith, standing a few paces away, felt the weight of each second passing. The stark reality of his actions bore down on him—his inability to control the celestial power had nearly cost Emma her life. He watched, tormented by guilt, as they applied salves and whispered incantations, the air thick with the scent of healing herbs and the low hum of ancient spells.

Aurelia, sensing Kaelith's despair, paused to address him. She shared a poignant memory of a time long past, drawing a parallel that she hoped would provide both guidance and solace. "There was a time," she began softly, ensuring her words reached only Kaelith, "when I faced a similar choice. Alex was mortally wounded, attacked by rogues when he was still mortal. My decision to save him by sharing my vampire essence was driven by love, a force so powerful that it led to our ascension."

Her story was a testament to the rare bonds that can form between immortals, bonds that defy the typical ennui of eternal life. "Our bond has endured through the centuries, not out of boredom but through a continuously deepening connection," she explained, hoping to illuminate the possibility of a profound commitment that could emerge from the trials they faced now.

This revelation hung in the air as Kaelith turned back to Emma. Her condition had stabilized slightly, but she was still perilously weak. He contemplated Aurelia's words, the weight of their meaning pressing upon him. The possibility of sparking Emma's ascension loomed large—a risk that could either save or destroy her.

Emma, barely conscious, her breaths shallow and pained, seemed to sense Kaelith's turmoil. As he approached, taking her hand gently in his, the connection they shared pulsed with a silent intensity. "Emma," he whispered, his voice thick with emotion, "I could try to help you ascend. It's risky, but it might be the only way to save you."

Her eyes fluttered open, meeting his with a clarity that belied her physical state. "Don't," she murmured faintly. "I'm scared, Kaelith. Not just of dying, but of losing what makes me... me. Our bond... it's rare. Let's not end it with a gamble."

Her words resonated deeply with Kaelith, reflecting the fear and love that intertwined between them. He nodded slowly, respecting her wish, feeling both relief and an acute sense of dread. Instead of using his blood, he stepped back, allowing Alex and Aurelia to continue their work. They mixed their blood with alchemical compounds, creating a potent blend that wouldn't spark ascension but might promote significant healing.

As they administered the mixture, Kaelith stood vigil by Emma's side, each of her labored breaths echoing in his heart. The room settled into a charged silence, every moment stretching as they waited to see if the treatment would take hold. Aurelia and Alex worked with a seamless efficiency, their actions a blend of medical expertise and vampiric power, their faces set in grim determination.

The night wore on, the tension never abating. Emma's fate hung in balance, a delicate thread that could sway with the slightest change. Kaelith, feeling the enormity of his powers and the consequences they wrought, realized the depth of his connection with Emma was something worth more than the vast expanse of his celestial abilities. It was a bond forged in adversity, strengthened by mutual respect and fear, and ultimately defined by the choices they made together.

As dawn approached, the first faint hints of light casting a pallid glow through the loft's windows, Emma's condition showed tentative signs of improvement. Her breathing became less labored, and the pallor of her skin gained a hint of warmth. Kaelith, exhausted but vigilant, remained by her side, his presence a silent promise of steadfast support no matter the outcome.

Chapter 8: Malachor's Gambit

The loft had become a place of recovery for Emma, but that fragile peace was shattered. Kaelith stood by the window, feeling a strange sense of calm. Since rescuing Emma, his control over his celestial abilities had become effortless, like a part of him had finally aligned. But that calm was about to be ripped apart.

A pressure in the air signaled danger, a malevolent force moving through the city—Malachor was coming.

The windows exploded inward without warning, shards of glass raining across the room as Malachor made his violent entrance. His body was marked with burns from the previous confrontation with Kaelith, his skin scorched and twisted in agony, but it hadn't diminished his thirst for power.

"You think you've mastered your celestial abilities, don't you?" Malachor sneered, his voice dripping with venom. "That power should belong to me!"

Kaelith stood tall, his wings unfurling. Light and shadow twisted around him in perfect balance, the brilliant radiance of his light reflecting off the broken glass, while the dark, ominous wings curled around him like a shield. "You'll never have it," Kaelith growled, his eyes glowing with fury.

Malachor's eyes flicked briefly toward Emma, and a cruel grin spread across his lips. "You should've killed her when you had the chance."

Kaelith's anger surged. His wings flared, and without hesitation, he charged at Malachor, his celestial power blazing around him. The impact was immediate, the force of their collision sending a shockwave through the room. Walls cracked, and the loft buckled under the strain as their powers clashed violently. Light flared from Kaelith's form, searing the air around him, while Malachor's dark energy twisted and churned, corrupting everything it touched.

"Alex, get her out of here!" Aurelia shouted. She and Alex moved quickly, supporting Emma between them as they hurried to the back of the loft. Kaelith gave a brief nod, his attention still locked on Malachor.

The moment they were clear, the battle erupted in full force.

Malachor lunged at Kaelith, his movements ferocious and wild, driven by his obsession to claim Kaelith's divine power. His fists collided with Kaelith's defenses, sending cracks through the floor beneath them. Kaelith pushed back, his wings slashing through the air with bursts of light and shadow that scorched and twisted the loft around them.

"You think you're worthy of ascension?" Malachor spat, his voice filled with venom as he launched another savage attack. "You're nothing but a weakling playing with power you don't understand!"

Kaelith blocked his strike, but the force sent him reeling back into the wall, smashing through plaster and beams. "You want ascension so badly?" Kaelith snarled, his voice laced with both fury and control. "You'll never have it."

Malachor's laugh was twisted, desperate. "I will take everything from you. I will ascend, Kaelith! You can't stop me!"

The fight tore through the loft, each blow a whirlwind of destruction. Glass shattered, furniture splintered, and the very walls groaned under the pressure. Kaelith summoned a surge of light, slamming Malachor back, but the dark warlord retaliated just as fiercely. His claws raked across Kaelith's chest, sending a ripple of dark energy into his core.

Pain shot through Kaelith, but he gritted his teeth and pushed forward, unleashing a burst of pure celestial light that sent Malachor skidding across the floor. The light burned into Malachor's already scorched skin, causing him to scream in agony, but his greed—his obsession—kept him fighting.

"Do you really think you've mastered that power?" Malachor roared, forcing himself back to his feet. His eyes glinted with hunger as he charged forward again, his body a blur of shadow and darkness.

Kaelith met him head-on. Their powers collided in a blinding explosion of light and shadow, the force sending shockwaves through the loft. They grappled, fists and wings crashing into each other with brutal intensity, neither willing to back down. Kaelith's control was calm and measured, but Malachor's rage made him relentless, each blow fueled by desperation.

The loft was reduced to wreckage around them. Windows shattered, beams cracked, and the very foundation of the building trembled under the strain. The battle was savage, unrelenting, as they tumbled through the apartment, smashing through walls, breaking everything in their path.

Kaelith's breath came in ragged bursts as he fought to maintain his control. Every strike he landed was filled with purpose, but Malachor kept coming, refusing to yield. The dark warlord was driven by one desire: ascension. He clawed at Kaelith's wings, trying to tear them apart, but Kaelith responded with a blast of shadow that sent Malachor reeling.

But Malachor wasn't finished. With a snarl, he hurled a sphere of dark energy at Kaelith, who barely managed to deflect it in time. The ball of energy smashed through the ceiling, sending debris raining down around them.

"You can't stop me, Kaelith," Malachor hissed, his voice laced with malice. "Your power will be mine!"

Kaelith raised his wings, both light and shadow coiling around him, ready to strike. The room crackled with energy as they prepared for the next assault, their powers building to another explosive clash.

Chapter 9: The Final Stand

The loft lay in ruins. Walls were crumbled, beams exposed, and shards of glass littered the floor, but the battle wasn't over. Kaelith stood in the center of the wreckage, his chest heaving from the brutal fight. His wings of light and shadow flared out behind him, burning with raw power. Malachor, still bearing the burns from their last confrontation, glared at him, eyes gleaming with hatred and hunger.

"You think you've won," Malachor spat, staggering forward. His skin sizzled where Kaelith's light had seared him, but it only seemed to fuel his rage. "You think you've mastered your power... but you're nothing!"

Kaelith said nothing, his glowing eyes locked onto Malachor. He had been pushed to his limits, and yet, he had never felt more in control of his celestial nature. But this fight wasn't over—not yet.

Malachor lunged with a savage roar, his movements fueled by desperation. Kaelith met him head-on, their bodies colliding with a force that shook the crumbling loft. Their fists clashed in a flurry of powerful strikes, every blow shattering what little remained of the walls around them. The sound of bone meeting bone echoed through the space as they fought like titans, locked in a brutal contest of strength and endurance.

Alex and Aurelia, having moved Emma to safety in the back room, now joined the fray. Immune to the light, their vampiric strength was unmatched. With a fierce battle cry, Alex tackled Malachor from the side, his fists landing solid hits on the warlord's scorched body.

"You'll never take his power!" Alex growled, punching Malachor in the ribs, his knuckles cracking against Malachor's burned skin.

Aurelia moved like a blur, striking with deadly precision. Her hands wrapped around a piece of broken steel from the shattered loft, using it as a makeshift weapon. She swung the metal at Malachor, the impact sending him staggering backward into the debris.

But Malachor wasn't finished. He snarled, pushing off the ground with renewed fury, launching himself at Kaelith once again. The force of his strike sent Kaelith crashing through what remained of a wall, collapsing the ceiling above them.

Kaelith's wings flared out just in time, catching the debris before it could crush him. With a powerful beat of his wings, he rose from the wreckage and slammed into Malachor, pinning him to the ground. His fist connected with Malachor's face, the force cracking the floor beneath them.

"You'll never have my power," Kaelith growled, his voice low and dangerous.

Malachor spat blood, his eyes wild with rage. "I'll rip it from you!" he howled, throwing Kaelith off him with a surge of adrenaline.

Kaelith landed hard but rolled to his feet just as Malachor charged again, this time with both hands outstretched, trying to choke the life out of him. Kaelith caught Malachor's wrists, their strength evenly matched as they struggled for dominance.

Alex was quick to strike again, slamming into Malachor from the side, breaking the deadlock. Malachor stumbled, and before he could regain his footing, Aurelia was on him, kicking him hard in the chest, sending him crashing into a support beam. The beam splintered under the impact, the entire loft groaning as more of the structure began to give way.

But Malachor didn't care. He rose again, blood dripping from his mouth, his skin blistering under the intense heat of Kaelith's light. The fight was taking its toll on him, but his obsession with ascension kept him going, kept him pushing forward despite his injuries.

"Don't you understand?" Malachor snarled, his voice hoarse. "Your power... it's wasted on you. You don't deserve it!" He threw a wild punch, which Kaelith dodged, countering with a blow that knocked Malachor back into the shattered remains of a window frame.

The sunlight was rising. The first golden rays of dawn spilled into the loft, illuminating the destruction. The curtains had long since been torn down, and now, with every window shattered, there was nothing to shield them from the inevitable.

Kaelith knew what was coming. The light from the rising sun grew stronger, and with it, his own power surged. His wings glowed brighter, the light and shadow intertwining perfectly around him. He saw Malachor begin to recoil as the sun's light touched his already burned skin.

Kaelith advanced on Malachor, determination burning in his eyes. "It's over, Malachor."

Malachor lashed out one last time, but his movements were slower now, his strength waning. Kaelith caught him by the throat, lifting him off the ground effortlessly. Malachor struggled, but it was futile. Kaelith's celestial form burned with the radiance of the sun itself, the light pouring through the broken windows combining with his own power.

Malachor screamed in pain as the sunlight seared his skin, his flesh cracking and blistering under the dual assault of the natural light and Kaelith's celestial glow. His body began to crumble, his screams turning into a guttural, desperate wail.

Kaelith walked toward the shattered edge of the loft, still holding Malachor by the scruff of his neck. "This is your end," Kaelith said, his voice calm but filled with finality.

The sunlight intensified, casting Malachor fully into its deadly embrace. His body writhed and burned, turning to ash as the light consumed him. Kaelith tightened his grip and with a final push, hurled Malachor through the broken window.

Malachor's body disintegrated as it hit the sunlight outside, his ashes scattering into the morning sky. His screams faded into the wind, leaving nothing but silence in their wake.

Kaelith stood there, bathed in the light of the rising sun, his wings of light and shadow still flared out behind him. His chest heaved with exhaustion, but he knew it was over. The battle had ended, and Malachor was no more.

The loft was destroyed, the building barely standing, but the fight had been won. Alex and Aurelia stepped forward, their expressions filled with both relief and awe at what they had just witnessed.

Kaelith lowered his wings, his celestial form dimming as he turned toward them. The weight of what had just happened, the toll it had taken, began to sink in. But for now, the only thing that mattered was that they had survived—and Malachor had not.

Chapter 10: Aftermath

Kaelith stood motionless at the edge of the broken window, his body bathed in the warm sunlight as it poured into the ruined loft. His wings of light and shadow began to retract, their brilliance fading as he slowly reverted back to his human form. The battle was over. Malachor was gone—defeated, his ashes scattered to the winds.

But the victory came with an unexpected weight. The loft was silent, save for the faint sound of the breeze through the shattered glass. Kaelith breathed deeply, allowing himself a moment of peace. The struggle between light and shadow within him had vanished, replaced by a perfect equilibrium. For the first time, he felt no resistance within himself. It was as if the two forces had finally come into perfect balance.

Then, a voice—soft, almost angelic—called to him from behind.

"Kaelith," the voice whispered.

He turned slowly, his breath catching in his throat. Emma stood there, fully healed. But this was more than just physical healing. Her skin shimmered faintly in the light, and her eyes, which had once reflected the hunger of a vampire, now shone with the radiance of something... more.

She stepped toward the sunlight streaming through the broken window, her eyes open to the bright rays, and for the first time, there was no pain. No fear. No hunger gnawing at her insides. Emma's lips parted in a soft smile, tears welling in her eyes as she looked at her mother and father, standing nearby.

"Is this what it's like?" she asked, her voice trembling with emotion.

Alex and Aurelia, standing at the edge of the room, were already moving toward her. They embraced their daughter, their faces etched with wonder and joy. Emma had ascended. She was no longer bound by the limitations of a vampire, no longer a slave to hunger or the need for blood. She had reached something beyond, something higher.

Emma then turned to Kaelith, her eyes filled with gratitude and love. She stepped closer to him, the air between them thick with unspoken emotion. Without hesitation, she wrapped her arms around him, pulling him into a deep, passionate kiss. The world seemed to stand still for a moment as they embraced, the chaos of the battle fading into the background.

When they pulled apart, there were no words needed. Their bond had grown deeper than either of them could have imagined.

A few days later...

The remnants of the loft had been cleared, but the scars of the battle remained. The world outside, though unchanged in appearance, felt different to Kaelith. He had won, yes, but the cost was great. His powers were now fully under his control, and the internal struggle between light and shadow was gone. He had achieved perfect balance. Yet, as he stood looking out over the city, a sense of uncertainty gnawed at him.

What was his place in this world now?

Kaelith knew that his journey wasn't over. The future remained unclear, and though the victory over Malachor had brought him peace for now, there were questions about what came next. And so, with that thought, he made his way to the Vampire Council.

The council chamber was silent as Kaelith entered, his presence commanding the room. The council members watched him closely, their faces a mix of fear and curiosity. Kaelith had proven himself to be more than they had ever anticipated—more powerful, more dangerous—but he was not there to fight.

"I will not be hunted or threatened again," Kaelith said, his voice firm and resolute. "Ascension is not mine to give. It is not something that can be taken. If any of you believe I have the power to grant it to you, know that it would only be temporary—an illusion. True ascension does not come from me. It comes from within."

The council members exchanged glances, their expressions uncertain. Kaelith continued.

"Ascension is a sacrifice of pure and abiding love. It is the willingness to give up your life, your well-being, for someone else—something greater than yourself. That is the only path to true ascension. No amount of power or hunger will bring you what you seek. If you remain closed-minded, if you continue to chase greed and control, you will never find ascension."

The room was tense as Kaelith finished speaking. His words carried the weight of truth, and the council knew it. They had sought power for centuries, but now they were faced with the realization that their path was wrong.

After a long silence, one of the elder council members stood. "We hear you, Kaelith," he said, his voice low. "And we agree."

The council, recognizing the wisdom in Kaelith's words, reached a quiet agreement. No more would they seek ascension through greed or manipulation. They would respect the boundaries Kaelith had set.

With that, Kaelith turned to leave the chamber, a sense of finality settling over him. His role in this world was far from over, but for now, there was peace.

As he stepped out into the night, Kaelith glanced up at the sky, his mind turning to Emma and the uncertain future they would face together.

Epilogue

The night stretched long and quiet, draped in the soft glow of the moon. The garden below the terrace was bathed in silver light, every leaf and petal catching the soft shimmer of nightfall. A gentle breeze stirred through the trees, carrying with it the faint scent of jasmine and something wilder, older. Kaelith stood at the edge of the terrace, leaning lightly on the stone railing, his eyes tracing the distant skyline where the city lights flickered like grounded stars. Everything felt still—a stillness that carried weight, like the world was breathing in unison with him.

He inhaled deeply, savoring the peace that had settled around him. This place had become a sanctuary of sorts, where the constant push and pull of life seemed to slow. The world, for now, was in balance, and Kaelith had found a rare moment where he wasn't chasing something—or being chased by it. The night was quiet, but it was not the same kind of quiet he had known in the past. This quiet felt earned, deserved. It felt like a beginning, not an end.

Footsteps broke the silence behind him, soft and measured. He knew the rhythm well. Emma appeared beside him, her presence as familiar as the moonlight. She had changed in so many ways, yet she still felt like the person he had come to trust above all others. Her long, dark hair caught the light as she stepped closer, her expression thoughtful but calm. She was different now, more grounded in her new existence. But there was still that fire in her, that quiet strength he had always admired.

Emma slid her hands into the pockets of her jacket, her gaze sweeping over the garden below. "You always find the quietest places," she mused, her voice carrying that soft, playful edge he had come to know so well.

Kaelith smiled faintly, his eyes never leaving the sky. "I think it's because I can finally enjoy them."

There was a subtle humor in his voice, but beneath it was something deeper—an understanding that the storms they had weathered together had finally given way to this: the peace of knowing who he was and what he had become.

Emma leaned against the railing beside him, her shoulder brushing his. "You were always chasing something before," she said, her tone reflective. "Now... I don't know. It feels like you've stopped running."

Kaelith considered her words for a moment, his eyes tracing the edges of the clouds drifting lazily overhead. "Maybe I have. Or maybe I've just stopped running from myself."

Emma didn't reply immediately. Instead, she turned her gaze upward, watching the stars. The air around them was thick with the kind of quiet that wasn't empty, but full. Full of possibility, full of questions, full of answers they hadn't yet asked.

For a long while, neither of them spoke. The sound of the wind through the trees, the distant hum of the city below, the soft rustle of leaves—it all wrapped around them, pulling them into the present. There were no battles to fight tonight, no enemies lurking in the shadows. There was only this—this strange, quiet moment of peace they hadn't known they needed.

After what felt like hours, Emma finally broke the silence. "Do you think it will stay like this?" she asked, her voice quieter now, almost hesitant. "This calm... this peace?"

Kaelith glanced at her, studying her face for a moment before turning his gaze back to the sky. "No," he said, his voice steady but filled with understanding. "It won't."

There was no sadness in his words, no fear. Just acceptance. The world never stayed still for long. Not for people like them.

Emma smiled softly, as if she had expected the answer but still needed to hear it aloud. "And are you ready for whatever comes next?"

Kaelith exhaled slowly, feeling the weight of the question settle in his chest. "I am," he said finally, his voice filled with certainty. "Whatever it is, I'm ready."

They stood together in the quiet, the moonlight casting long shadows across the stone beneath their feet. Emma shifted slightly, turning so that her shoulder pressed lightly against his arm, a small but significant gesture. It wasn't often that she allowed herself to be vulnerable, even in moments of peace. But this was different. They were different now.

For a moment, Kaelith closed his eyes, letting the breeze wash over him, grounding him in the present. The peace they had found here wasn't fragile, but it wasn't permanent either. He knew that, and so did Emma. But that didn't make it any less meaningful. They had learned to savor these moments, to live in them without worrying about what would come next.

"I never thought we'd get to this point," Emma said after a long pause, her voice barely more than a whisper.

Kaelith turned to look at her, catching the faint shimmer of emotion in her eyes. "Neither did I," he admitted. "But here we are."

Emma's gaze lingered on his for a moment longer before she turned her attention back to the garden below. "Do you think... Do you think we'll ever really be done with all of this?" she asked, her tone thoughtful but uncertain. "The fighting, the running... the constant need to survive?"

Kaelith considered the question carefully, his mind turning over the possibilities, the unknowns. "I don't know if it'll ever be truly over," he said finally, his voice calm. "But I think we've found something better. Something worth fighting for."

Emma nodded slowly, her expression softening. "I like that answer," she said quietly. "It feels... honest."

Kaelith smiled, a small, genuine smile that came more easily now than it ever had before. "I've had enough lies to last me a lifetime. I'd rather be honest."

The night deepened around them, the stars growing brighter as the city below dimmed. The world felt vast and unknowable, but for the first time, Kaelith felt at peace with that uncertainty. Whatever came next, whatever challenges or battles lay ahead, he knew he wouldn't face them alone.

They stayed on the terrace for hours, the moon rising higher in the sky, the night stretching out before them like a promise. Neither of them knew what the future would bring, but for now, that didn't matter. They had each other. They had peace. And they had time.

For now, that was enough.

Don't miss out!

Visit the website below and you can sign up to receive emails whenever Edward Heath publishes a new book. There's no charge and no obligation.

https://books2read.com/r/B-A-WXZX-OQFBF

BOOKS 2 READ

Connecting independent readers to independent writers.

Did you love *Ascension*? Then you should read *Rebirth*[1] by Edward Heath!

Kaelith, a being born from the forbidden union of an angel and a demon, finds himself in a world where he does not belong. Raised in the mortal realm, he possesses unique abilities to manipulate light and shadow, hinting at his celestial heritage. As Kaelith grows, he is haunted by visions of a past life—battles and a warrior's legacy that seem to belong to Damu, a legendary figure revered and feared in vampire lore as the father of vampires.

Navigating his complex powers and the memories of a soul he carries but does not fully understand, Kaelith struggles with his identity and the heavy burden of his origin. His journey of self-discovery brings him into the hidden enclaves of vampires and the secretive councils that govern

---

1. https://books2read.com/u/4NV8q6

2. https://books2read.com/u/4NV8q6

the supernatural, where he learns more about his mysterious abilities and the balance of light and dark within him.

Faced with the truth of his existence and the echoes of a past life, Kaelith must decide his path. Will he embrace the legacy left by the soul within him, or will he forge a new path, one that transcends the dichotomy of heavenly grace and infernal power? "The New Path" is a tale of self-discovery, legacy, and the eternal struggle between light and darkness, inviting readers into a world where the lines between good and evil are blurred, and the journey to understand one's true nature is fraught with conflict and intrigue.

Read more at https://twitter.com/Iam8lu3.

Also by Edward Heath

Beyond
Beyond Belonging
Beyond the Boundaries
The Adventures of Nance Hatfield
Journey Through the Stars
The Nexus
The Veiled Expanse
Beyond the Edge

Bloodstained Shadows
A BloodStained Shadow
A BloodStained War
BloodStained Beginnings
Blood Ronin
Viking Blood
BloodStained Tears
BloodStained Eclipse
A Midnight Wedding
Blood Bound
Blood Doll
Bloodstained Moon
Enchanted Bonds

Legacy of Shadows

Midnight Carnival
Midnight Carnival
Midnight Carnival The Enchanted Forest
Midnight Carnival: The Maze of Shadows
Midnight Carnival and the Haunted Masquerade
Midnight Carnival The Beginning

Redemptions
The Judgment of Gabriel Hawke
The Redemption of Matthew Hawke

Shadow Banned
Shadow Banned

Shadows Reborn
Ascension
Afterlife
Rebirth
Rebirth

The Hunt
In the Shadow of the Hunt
The Hunt: Into the Frost

The Hunt Sands of Survival
The Hunt
Echoes of Balance
I Dream
Utopia Sold, Dystopia Lived

Standalone
Evil Bunny
Wild Inferno
Beyond Absurdity
Requiem: Shadow and Light
The Garden Gnome
Pain
Smoke and Shadows
The Chosen
Shattered Democracy
Shadows of Valor
Breaking Stupid
Alien Ultimatum
Luck o' the Unlucky
Medusa
Fluffy the Demon Destroyer of the Worlds

Watch for more at https://twitter.com/Iam8lu3.

About the Author

Edward Heath, a passionate digital artist and book publisher, is committed to an open-minded approach in the arts.My focus is on nurturing diverse talents and bringing unique perspectives.**https://linktr.ee/IamBlu3https://X.com/Iam8lu3**
Read more at https://twitter.com/Iam8lu3.

Milton Keynes UK
Ingram Content Group UK Ltd.
UKHW040639131024
449481UK00001B/64